Walking Between the Worlds

A Journey with Hecate

Written and Illustrated by

VUGHIR
Vesperra
MORRIGAN

This is a work of fiction. Similarities to real people, places, or events are entirely coincidental.

WALKING BETWEEN THE WORLDS: A JOURNEY WITH HECATE

First edition. November 20, 2024.

Copyright © 2024 Vespera Morrigan.

ISBN: 979-8230482857

Written by Vespera Morrigan.

Table of Contents

Title Page..1

Thank you and Dedication to My Daughters..................................9

Syllabus for Walking Between the Worlds: A Journey with Hecate 11

Opening Prayer: A Call to Rise 17

A Prayer to Begin the Journey..19

Offerings at the Crossroads 21

Ritual: Opening the Way 23

Light is powerful 25

Chapter 3: The Dark Moon's Embrace 27

A Ritual for the Dark Moon: Shadow Work..................................29

An Offering to the Spirits 31

The Ritual of Safe Passage 35

The Maiden 39

The Mother 41

The Crone 43

A Spell to Unlock Your Magic..45

A Ritual of Descent..47

The Guardians of the Crossroads 51

The Ritual of the Wild Hunt: Embracing Your Fate.......................55

A Prayer to the Black Dog for Guidance 59

A Feast for the Hounds 63

A Dedication Ritual to Hecate as Goddess of Witches 65

Hecate's Sacred Herbs..69

A Potion of Protection 71

Moon Magic and Scrying...73

The Crossroads Spread 77

The Light in the Darkness 79

A Ritual to Invoke Hecate's Torches..81

A Prayer for Inner Wisdom 83

A Crossroads Ritual for Clarity..87

A Meditation on the Eternal Flame..91

The Elements of Hecate's Altar...93

Steps to Building the Altar 95

Deities That Align Well with Hecate 99

Deities Best Kept Separate...101

Creating a Harmonious Shared Altar...103

Key Symbols of Hecate.. 107

A Ritual of Symbolic Invocation 113

Hecate's Protection: The Fierce Guardian........................ 115

The Sacred Oath 117

Walking Hecate's Path: Who Should Follow 119

The Qualities of Hecate's Followers.................................. 121

How to Walk Hecate's Path.. 123

The Path of Sacred Devotion 125

A Special Note to My Dearest Husband 127

Vespera Morrigan | About the Author: Vespera Morrigan 129

At the crossroads of shadow and light, where the seen and unseen converge, she stands, Hecate, keeper of the torches, guardian of mysteries, and guide through the veils of the worlds.

Thank you and Dedication to My Daughters

I dedicate this work to my four beautiful daughters: follower of Persephone, follower of Hecate, follower of Nyx, and last but certainly not least, follower of Loki. You have chosen the path less traveled, questioning the world around you and courageously forging your own way. Your strength, curiosity, and wisdom fill me with pride every day. May Hecate's torches always light your way as you seek knowledge and walk with courage through the crossroads of life. I am so proud of each of you for your bravery and integrity, for refusing to accept easy answers and daring to question everything.

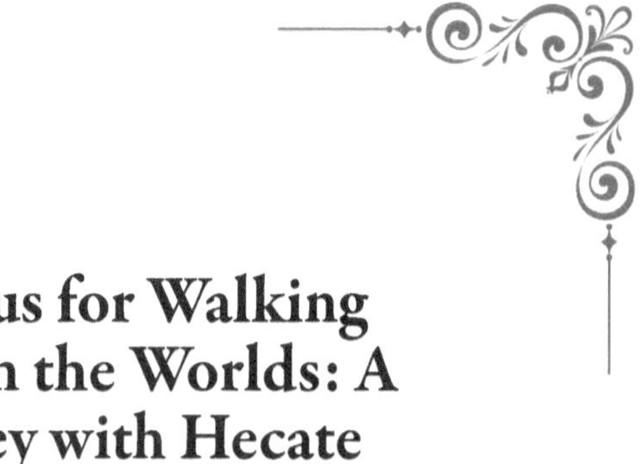

Syllabus for Walking Between the Worlds: A Journey with Hecate

By Vespera Morrigan

Chapter 1: Hecate, Queen of the Crossroads

IN THIS CHAPTER, WE explore Hecate's role as the goddess of transitions, thresholds, and the powerful symbolism of the crossroads. Discover how the crossroads hold magical significance and how to harness their energy in your spiritual practice.

Chapter 2: Hecate's Sacred Symbols

AN INTRODUCTION TO the key symbols of Hecate, including her torches, keys, hounds, and the Strophalos. Each symbol is imbued with meaning and power, offering insight into her complex nature and how to work with her through these sacred icons.

Chapter 3: The Dark Moon and Hecate

HECATE'S CONNECTION to the dark moon and the cycles of the moon reveal her dominion over hidden realms and transformation. This chapter explores the moon's phases and how they influence Hecate's magic and the rituals performed in her name.

Chapter 4: Hecate, Guide of Souls

DELVE INTO HECATE'S role as a psychopomp, guiding souls through the transitions of life and death. Understand her connection to the underworld and how to work with her energy for protection and guidance in navigating life's transitions.

Chapter 5: The Triple Goddess: Maiden, Mother, Crone

HECATE'S TRIPLE FORM encompasses all stages of life—birth, life, and death. Explore the symbolism of Hecate as Maiden, Mother, and Crone, and how these archetypes reflect her power over the past, present, and future.

Chapter 6: Working with Hecate in Daily Practice

LEARN HOW TO INCORPORATE Hecate's energy into your daily life through devotion, rituals, and offerings. Simple practices are shared to strengthen your connection with the goddess.

Chapter 7: Honoring the Dead and Ancestral Magic

HECATE'S LINK TO THE dead and her guidance in honoring ancestors is explored. This chapter offers rituals for ancestral reverence and magic, connecting you to your lineage and those who came before.

Chapter 8: Hecate's Role as the Protector of Witches

HECATE IS KNOWN AS the guardian of witches. This chapter dives into her fierce protection and how to call upon her for defense, guidance, and empowerment in your magical practice.

Chapter 9: Divination in Hecate's Light

HECATE'S CONNECTION to divination is discussed in this chapter, with guidance on working with tarot, scrying, and other forms of divination under her influence.

Chapter 10: Rituals for the Crossroads

LEARN POWERFUL RITUALS for invoking Hecate's guidance at the crossroads of life, whether literal or metaphorical. Understand how the energy of the crossroads can aid in decision-making and transformation.

Chapter 11: Hecate's Torches of Illumination

HECATE'S TORCHES REPRESENT more than just light—they symbolize knowledge, clarity, and the ability to see through the veils of illusion. Learn how to invoke her torches in times of uncertainty.

Chapter 12: The Keys of Hecate

AS THE KEEPER OF KEYS, Hecate holds the power to open doors to knowledge, opportunity, and spiritual realms. This chapter explores the symbolism of the key in rituals and devotion to her.

Chapter 13: Hecate, Goddess of Witches

AN EXPLORATION OF HECATE'S deep connection to witchcraft and how she empowers those who walk the path of the witch.

Chapter 14: The Sacred Herbs of Hecate

HECATE IS ALSO THE goddess of the earth and its sacred plants. This chapter delves into the magical properties of the herbs sacred to her and how to use them in spellwork and rituals.

Chapter 15: Divination in Hecate's Light

EXPLORE HOW TO WORK with Hecate through divination, using scrying, tarot, and the moon's phases to receive her wisdom and guidance.

Chapter 16: Hecate's Tarot Spread

A SPECIAL TAROT SPREAD inspired by Hecate's three faces, designed to guide you through the choices, challenges, and transformations in your life.

Chapter 17: Hecate's Torches of Illumination

HOW HECATE'S TORCHES not only light the physical path but also illuminate the inner world, offering wisdom through dark times.

Chapter 18: The Flame of Inner Wisdom

DISCOVER HOW HECATE'S light leads you to the wisdom that resides within, helping you to embrace your true self and the power of transformation.

Chapter 19: The Torches and the Crossroads

A DEEPER LOOK INTO the significance of Hecate's torches at the crossroads and how they guide us through important decisions in life.

Chapter 20: The Eternal Flame

HECATE'S ETERNAL FLAME burns through the cycles of life, death, and rebirth. This chapter explores the symbolism of her eternal light.

Chapter 21: Creating Hecate's Altar

A GUIDE TO CREATING a sacred altar for Hecate, filled with her symbols and offerings. Learn how to create a space that honors her presence.

Chapter 22: Sharing Hecate's Altar

EXPLORE HOW HECATE shares her sacred space with other deities and which gods or goddesses align well with her energy on a shared altar.

Chapter 23: The Sacred Symbols of Hecate

DIVE INTO THE KEY SYMBOLS of Hecate, including the key, torches, crossroads, dogs, and the serpent, and how they can be used in rituals.

Chapter 24: Incorporating Hecate's Symbols into Rituals

LEARN HOW TO INTEGRATE Hecate's symbols into your rituals and magical practices for a deeper connection with her

Introduction

In the stillness of the night, when the moon hangs high, and the shadows stretch long, a flame flickers in the distance. This is the light of Hecate, the ancient goddess of magic, the crossroads, and the unseen realms. For centuries, her presence has guided those brave enough to walk the paths of transformation, wisdom, and mystery. She stands at the threshold between worlds, holding her torches aloft, offering her light to those who seek to journey beyond the known. To follow Hecate is to embrace both light and shadow, to understand that within every dark place, there is truth, and within every challenge, there is growth. She is the protector of witches, the guide of souls, and the keeper of the keys that unlock the deepest mysteries of life, death, and rebirth.

This book is an invitation to step onto her path, to explore her magic, her symbols, and her wisdom. It is a transformative journey through the realms she guards—a journey that will not only challenge you but also empower you, transform you, and reveal the hidden truths that lie within your own soul.

As you walk between the worlds with Hecate, you will discover that her power is not distant but ever-present. Her torches burn for you, lighting the way through the darkness. Her wisdom is here, waiting to be uncovered, for those who dare to seek it. This is not just a journey, but a personal connection with Hecate.

May this book be your guide as Hecate guides us all—through the crossroads, through the shadows, and toward the flame of inner wisdom that burns within each of us.

Opening Prayer: A Call to Rise

You stand at the crossroads,
The place where all paths meet.
I have seen you there,
And now, you have chosen.
I am Hecate, the Keeper of the Keys,
The Guardian of the Threshold,
And I welcome you to walk my sacred path.
In the light of my torches, rise.
Rise as a seeker of truth,
A walker between worlds,
A bearer of my flame.
With this key, I unlock the door before you.
You will face darkness,
But you will not fear it,
For I will be there, my light guiding you.
As you rise, you will see through the veil,
The mysteries hidden in shadow will be yours to uncover.
The wisdom of life, death, and rebirth shall flow through you,
And the power of transformation will be yours.
Know that as you walk this path, you are mine.
I will protect you,
I will guide you,
And I will challenge you to become all that you are meant to be.

Chapter 1: The Crossroads Beckon

The night is dark, and the air is thick with mystery as you stand at the crossroads. The moon's pale glow bathes the world in silver, casting long shadows in your path. You can feel her presence — it's subtle at first, a faint whisper carried on the wind, a flicker at the corner of your vision. Then, like a warm, protective cloak, it wraps around you, comforting and unsettling.

"Are you ready?" the ancient and eternal voice asks.

You nod, unsure if you're responding to the wind or something more significant. A raven caws in the distance, and you feel a shiver down your spine.

I am Hecate, the Keeper of Keys, Guardian of the Threshold, Goddess of the In-Between. You have called, and I have come.

Hecate stands before you now, her dark robes flowing like water, her face partially hidden in shadow. She is neither entirely kind nor cruel, neither dark nor light — she is all things and yet none of them. She embodies balance, the eternal flow between life and death, beginnings and endings. And you, dear traveler, have stepped onto her path.

"I am the one who walks between worlds," she says, her voice filling the air with an electric hum. "And now you will walk with me."

A Prayer to Begin the Journey

Before you begin any work with me, call upon my name, for I am the torchbearer who illuminates the way:

"Hecate, Keeper of the Keys, Queen of Night, Guide me through the darkness. Light my path and guard my steps. You who stand at the Crossroads open the gates to wisdom and power. I honor you with this offering of my heart, mind, and soul. Walk with me, O Great Hecate, as I walk the path of the Witch."

Offerings at the Crossroads

Hecate reminds us that offerings are meaningful, not because of what is offered, but because of the intention behind them.

Honey to sweeten her presence in your life.

Garlic to ward off negative energy and spirits.

Eggs are symbols of rebirth and new beginnings.

Red wine is poured on the ground to honor the blood of life and death.

A key, a symbol of trust in her guidance, left behind at the crossroads as a token of your journey.

"Place your gifts here," she says, gesturing toward the ground where the paths meet. "And do not turn around after you've given your offering. The past is no longer important to you."

Ritual: Opening the Way

As you move forward, she gives you a torch. Its flame dances with an ethereal light, illuminating the way ahead. The ceremony she leads you through is uncomplicated yet deeply meaningful.

Select a key that holds personal significance. It could be an old key you've kept from a forgotten lock or one that symbolizes something you want to unlock in your life.

At midnight, visit a crossroads. Clasp the key firmly in your hands and invoke Hecate:

"Hecate, Guardian of the Crossroads, I seek your guidance. Open the doors to wisdom, magic, and enigmas that lie beyond. Guide me to the path I am meant to tread."

Afterward, bury the key at the base of the crossroads. This act represents your readiness to leave the past behind, embrace the unknown, and trust Hecate to lead you. Please light a candle and let it burn as you depart without looking back.

Chapter 2: The Torches of Wisdom

"Light is powerful," Hecate says softly as her torch burns beside you. "It casts away shadows, but it also creates them. Where there is light, there is darkness. Do you see?"

In this section, we will delve into the idea of duality. Hecate embodies the liminal spaces, the places in between where most fear to tread. She teaches that embracing both sides of ourselves — the light and the dark — is essential for personal growth and power.

Hecate shares her ancient knowledge through whispered teachings, prayers, rituals, and personal anecdotes that relate to historical references and her connection to the world of magic. Each chapter dives deeper into her mysteries—the moon phases, herbs, divination, and the underworld—while also keeping the reader engaged with practical advice on how to work with her energy.

Prayers and invocations will be woven throughout, offering moments of reflection and spiritual connection. Offerings and rituals will be placed at critical points, urging the reader to develop a deeper relationship with the goddess.

The goal will be to maintain a conversational, almost narrative tone — as if Hecate herself were leading the reader through a journey, step by step, and guiding them to find their power.

Light is powerful

At every crossroad, the flames of her torches light the paths, but it is the seeker who must choose which one to walk."

Chapter 3: The Dark Moon's Embrace

The moon has vanished from the sky, shrouded in darkness. This is the time of the dark moon — a moment of pause, of stillness, when the earth holds its breath before the next cycle begins. Hecate smiles, her eyes gleaming in the blackness.

"This is when my power is at its peak," she whispers, her voice like silk. "The dark moon is a time of reflection, of turning inward. It is when you must confront your shadows."

You stand in silence with her, feeling the stillness around you, the absence of light. But there is no fear, for Hecate is here, her presence strong and unwavering. She teaches you that darkness is not something to be feared, but embraced. It is within the dark that the seeds of creation stir. It is within the void that true transformation occurs.

Those who walk with Hecate are never truly alone, for her torches burn beside them, casting light in the darkest of times."

A Ritual for the Dark Moon: Shadow Work

To honor Hecate during the dark moon, and to work with her energy, we must begin by acknowledging the parts of ourselves that we keep hidden — our shadows. The following ritual is designed to help you delve into your inner darkness, to face it with courage, and to emerge stronger on the other side.

You will need:

A black candle

A small mirror

A journal and pen

Mugwort or sage for cleansing

An offering of dark bread or wine

Begin by cleansing your space with mugwort or sage. Light the black candle, allowing its flame to be the only source of illumination. Sit quietly in front of the mirror, gazing into your own eyes.

"Hecate, guide me as I walk through my shadow. Help me to see what I have hidden, and give me the strength to face it."

Take a few deep breaths and, when you are ready, begin to write. Reflect on your fears, your regrets, your insecurities. What parts of yourself have you buried deep within? As you write, imagine Hecate standing beside you, her torch illuminating the corners of your soul. Once you have finished, read over your words. Do not judge them. Simply observe. Thank Hecate for her guidance and offer her the bread or wine as a symbol of your gratitude.

End the ritual by saying

"Hecate, Queen of Shadows, I honor you this night. I walk with you through the dark and find my strength within. As the moon returns, so shall I, reborn and renewed."

Blow out the candle, leaving the offering at the crossroads or another sacred space.

Chapter 4: The Keys to the Underworld

"Hecate holds the power over both life and death. As she turns the ancient brass key in her hand, she offers to share the wisdom of her ancestors and the knowledge of the underworld with those who seek it. She teaches that the realm of the dead is not to be feared but rather a place of learning, where the spirits of the departed wait to impart their stories and teachings to those willing to listen. With Hecate's guidance, one can learn to traverse between the two worlds.

An Offering to the Spirits

To honor Hecate and the spirits of the underworld, create a sacred altar. This can be a small space, set with intention and reverence, where you invite the presence of your ancestors and those who have passed.

You will need:
A black cloth to cover the altar
Photos or objects representing your ancestors
A skull or bones, symbolic of death
A bowl of salt for protection
A silver key to honor Hecate
An offering of pomegranates, wine, or bread
Once the altar is set, light a black or red candle and say:
"Hecate, Keeper of the Keys, I call upon you. Open the gates between the worlds and allow me to commune with the spirits of the dead. Ancestors, I honor you. I seek your wisdom, your guidance, and your strength."
Spend time in silence, meditating on the spirits who come to you. You may feel their presence as warmth in the air, a whisper in the wind, or simply a deep knowing. Listen to what they have to say and thank them for their wisdom. Leave the offering on the altar overnight.

Chapter 5: Walking with the Dead

As your journey with Hecate deepens, so too does your understanding
of death. "Do not fear it," she says in a low and calm voice. "For death
is but another threshold, another key to unlock."

In this chapter, we will explore Hecate's role as a psychopomp who
guides souls to the underworld. She is the torchbearer who leads the
dead across the threshold, ensuring safe passage to the other side. But
she is also a guardian, protecting the living from the restless spirits
who may wander too close.

The Ritual of Safe Passage

When someone you love passes, you can call upon Hecate to guide their soul safely to the other side. This ritual can be performed shortly after death or during remembrance, such as Samhain or the anniversary of their passing.

You will need:

A white candle symbolizes the soul's purity

A coin, representing payment for the ferryman

A critical symbolizing Hecate's guidance

A photo or item belonging to the deceased

Begin by lighting the white candle and placing the coin and key beside it. Hold the photo or item of the deceased in your hands and say:

"Hecate, Psychopomp, I call upon you. Guide the soul of [name] safely to the underworld. May they find peace and rest in the realm of the dead. I offer this coin as payment for the ferryman and this key as a token of trust in your guidance."

Take a few moments to be quiet and contemplate the given text—the deceased's life—and send them love and peace. Then, blow out the candle, leaving the coin and key as offerings at a crossroads or a graveyard.

Hecate will lead you through more profound initiations, complex rituals, and personal reflections on walking the witch's path. Each chapter will build upon the last, weaving together historical lore, modern witchcraft practices, and individual spiritual development.

The book will be filled with prayers, invocations, meditations, and rituals that offer practical and mystical ways to connect with Hecate's energy. Each section will feel like a new lesson, a personal guide from the goddess herself, as she teaches the reader to embrace their power and walk confidently between the worlds.

Chapter 6: The Three Faces of Hecate

As you walk with Hecate, you see her in her many forms. She is not just one goddess, but three — the Maiden, the Mother, and the Crone. These are not separate beings but aspects of a singular, powerful force. Hecate is time, the cycle of life, death, and rebirth. She wears each face depending on what lesson she has come to teach.

"You will meet all of me on this path," she says, her voice shifting like the wind. "In each face, there is a different truth. But all are part of the same wisdom."

The Maiden

The first face you encounter is the Maiden. She stands at the threshold of life, young and full of potential, a bright light in the darkness. With her, you feel the thrill of beginnings, the spark of curiosity that fuels your journey.

"I am the beginning," she whispers, her eyes full of promise. "I am the spark that ignites the fire of your soul."

The Maiden represents new growth, potential, and possibilities yet unrealized. In this form, Hecate encourages you to explore the unknown and to be bold and fearless in your pursuit of magic and self-discovery.

A Prayer to the Maiden

"Hecate of the new moon, shining in your youth, guide me on the path of beginnings. Light my way as I walk forward into the unknown. Please give me the courage to take risks, the wisdom to trust my instincts, and the strength to face the challenges ahead. I honor you, Maiden of the Crossroads, with this offering of flowers and honey, as sweet and fresh as the dawn."

Leave offerings of fresh flowers and honey for the Maiden, symbolizing growth and renewal. These offerings can be placed at a sacred space in nature or a personal altar dedicated to the energy of new beginnings.

The Mother

As you continue, Hecate transforms before your eyes. Now she is the Mother, the nurturer and protector, full of wisdom and life-giving energy. Her presence is comforting, but there is also a fierce strength behind her gentleness.

"I am the keeper of life," she says softly. "I nourish, protect, and defend those who walk my path."

The Mother represents the fullness of life, creation, and the nurturing force that sustains all living things. She reminds you of your power to create, not just in the physical sense but in your ability to shape the world around you through your intentions and actions.

A Prayer to the Mother

"Hecate, Great Mother, you who nurture and protect, be with me now. Please help me to grow in wisdom, to create with intention, and to give of myself freely. I offer this bread and wine to honor the life-giving force within you and me. Watch over me as I walk this path, and guide me with your loving strength."

Offer bread and wine to the Mother, symbols of sustenance and life. You may perform this ritual at home or near a body of water, connecting with the life force that flows through all things.

The Crone

Finally, you stand before the Crone. She is older now, her face lined with the marks of time, but her eyes are full of ancient wisdom. She holds the keys to the mysteries of death and transformation, the power to end and begin again.

"I am the end," she says, her voice like the wind rustling through dry leaves. "But in every ending, there is a new beginning."

The Crone is the final stage of life, the wise woman who knows the underworld's secrets. She teaches you that death is not to be feared but embraced as a natural part of the cycle. She is the gatekeeper to the otherworld, holding the keys to transformation and rebirth.

A Prayer to the Crone

"Hecate, Wise Crone, you who stand at the threshold of life and death, guide me through the dark places of my soul. Please help me to let go of what no longer serves and embrace the endings that lead to new beginnings. I honor you with this offering of pomegranates, symbols of death and rebirth. Walk with me through the shadows, and show me the wisdom in the darkness."

Leave pomegranates as an offering to the Crone, honoring her role as the keeper of death and rebirth. This offering can be made at a crossroads or graveyard, where Hecate's energy is vital.

Chapter 7: The Keys to Magic

As Hecate walks beside you, she hands you a key. It is old and tarnished, but you can feel its power humming beneath your fingertips. "This is not just any key," she says, "but the key to magic itself."

She explains that magic is not about wielding power over others or manipulating the world to one's will. It is about unlocking the hidden doors within yourself, finding the strength to walk your path, and aligning yourself with the forces of the universe.

"The greatest magic," she says, "is the magic of self-discovery."

A Spell to Unlock Your Magic

This spell is designed to help you unlock your inner power and find the courage to step fully into your magic. It is a simple spell, but its effects can be profound.

You will need:

A minor key (one you can wear as a charm or keep on your altar)

A black candle

A piece of parchment and a pen

A bowl of salt for protection

A mirror

Begin by cleansing your space with salt, creating a circle of protection around you. Light the black candle and hold the key in your hand. Look into the mirror, gazing deeply into your own eyes.

"Hecate, Keeper of Keys, I ask for your guidance. Help me unlock the doors within myself to find the magic hidden in my soul's depths."

On the parchment, write down what you wish to unlock within yourself. This could be a hidden talent, a new opportunity, or the strength to face a challenge. Once you have written it down, hold the key over the paper and say:

"With this key, I unlock my power. With Hecate's guidance, I walk the path of magic and self-discovery. So mote it be."

Keep the key as a symbol of your inner magic. You may wear it as a charm or place it on your altar as a reminder of your power.

Chapter 8: The Gates of the Underworld

Hecate smiles as you approach the gates of the underworld. You have walked with her for some time now, and she believes you are ready to face the deepest mysteries of life and death.

"Are you prepared to step through?" she asks, torch flickering in the shadows.

You nod, though your heart pounds in your chest. The gates loom before you, dark and imposing. But with Hecate beside you, there is nothing to fear.

A Ritual of Descent

This ritual is designed to help you connect with the underworld, face your fears, and emerge transformed. It is powerful and should be done with deep respect and intention.

You will need:

A black cloak or veil

A candle to represent Hecate's torch

A key to symbolize the gates of the underworld

A bowl of water to represent the river Styx

Begin by placing the key at your feet, symbolizing the gate you will cross. Light the candle and say:

"Hecate, Keeper of the Gates, guide me as I descend into the underworld. Help me to face the shadows and return with wisdom and strength."

Place the cloak or veil over your head, covering your eyes as you imagine stepping through the gates. In your mind's eye, see yourself descending into the darkness, feeling the presence of the spirits around you. Spend time in this space, asking Hecate to reveal what you need to know.

When you are ready, remove the veil and say:"

With Hecate's guidance, I have walked through the darkness. I return now, stronger and wiser, reborn in the light of her torch."

End the ritual by pouring the water from the bowl into the earth, honoring the connection between life and death.

⟡

Chapter 9: The Hounds of Hecate

As the moon rises high in the night sky, you hear the distant baying of dogs. Their howls echo through the air, growing closer with each passing moment. Hecate smiles softly, and beside her, spectral hounds appear, their eyes glowing like embers in the darkness. These are her sacred companions, the guardians of the threshold.

"Do you hear them?" she asks, her voice quiet yet powerful. "They have always been with me. My hounds see what others cannot, sense what others fear, and guard the way."

Hecate's dogs have long been associated with her role as a protector of travelers, especially those journeying through the liminal spaces between life and death. They are not just companions; they are fierce guardians, instilling a sense of security as they guide souls along the paths of the underworld and watch over the witches who call upon them.

The Guardians of the Crossroads

The dogs of Hecate guard the crossroads, where the veil between worlds is most tenuous. On consecrated crossroads, her devotion guards dogs against those seeking communion with spirits, protecting them and leading them through the unseen realms. "I charge you with the care of my dogs," she affirms, "Watching over, guiding, and revealing mysteries beyond."

A Prayer for the Protection of Hecate's Hounds

If you wish to have physical, emotional, or spiritual protection, you can invoke Hecate's hounds to watch over you. Loyal to the goddess, they extend that loyalty to those in her keeping, and their power is beyond compare.

You will need:

A small bone or figurine to represent Hecate's hounds

A white or black candle

A piece of onyx or obsidian for protection

Light the candle and place the bone or figurine in front of you. Hold the stone in your hand and close your eyes. Imagine immediately that Hecate's dogs are circling you, their eyes in glowing orbs in the dark, ready to protect and defend.

"Hecate, I invoke thy dogs of might. Protectors of crossroads, guardians of the way, surround me with thine presence. Keep me from harm and convey me safely around dark places. By thy powers and the faithfulness of thine hounds, I am safe.

Place the stone on your altar or carry it with you as a symbol of their protection. The bone or figure may be left at a crossroads as an offering to Hecate and her hounds, a return thanks for guidance.

Chapter 10: The Wild Hunt and the Howling Wind

In the deepest parts of the night, when the air grows still and the world holds its breath, a sound stirs the soul — the wild, untamed howl of Hecate's dogs as they ride the wind, leading the Wild Hunt. Hecate is not just the guardian of the dead but the hunt's leader, Hunting restless souls through the night.

"Do you feel the wind?" she asks, her eyes shining fiercely. "My

hounds ride the storm, chasing down those who flee from their fate."
The Wild Hunt is an ancient and powerful force, a spectral procession
of souls and spirits guided by Hecate and her hounds. It is said that
those who hear the howls of her dogs should take heed — the Hunt
Hunts not just for the dead but for those who are running from their
destiny.

The Ritual of the Wild Hunt: Embracing Your Fate

This ritual is for those who seek to embrace their fate to stop running from the challenges or transformations that lie ahead. Hecate's hounds will help you find the strength to face whatever is chasing you and to meet your fate with courage.

You will need:

A black candle

A piece of parchment and a pen

A dog figurine or image

A bell to symbolize the call of the Hunt

Huntn by lighting the black candle. Hold the dog figurine in your hand, connecting with the energy of Hecate's hounds. On the parchment, write down the things you have been running from — fears, challenges, changes that you have resisted. As you write, you may hear the distant howls of the Hunt Huntour mind's ear, urging you to face what you have been avoiding.

Ring the bell three times, calling the Hunt Huntour side.

"Hecate, leader of the Wild Hunt, I call upon your hounds. Chase away my fears, my doubts, and my hesitation. Please help me to face my fate with courage and to embrace the changes that lie ahead. By the power of your hounds, I meet my destiny."

Let the candle burn down and bury the parchment at a crossroads or in the earth, symbolizing the release of your fears and your acceptance of the path ahead.

Chapter 11: The Black Dog as a Guide

While Hecate's hounds are fierce protectors, one figure stands out among them—the Black Dog. Throughout history, the black dog has been recognized as a symbol of both fear and protection. It often appears at crossroads or graveyards, where the boundaries between life and death blur. In many cultures, the Black Dog is a psychopomp, guiding the souls of the dead safely to the afterlife.

"I am the Black Dog," Hecate says, her voice deep and resonant. In her form as the Black Dog, Hecate serves as both a guardian and a mentor, guiding those in search of her insight safely through the darkness. If you ever feel disoriented or unsure, you can invoke her in this guise to lead you back to your intended course.

A Prayer to the Black Dog for Guidance

When you find yourself standing at a metaphorical crossroads, unsure which direction to take, the Black Dog can guide you. This prayer will help you connect with Hecate in her form as the Black Dog and ask for her guidance through uncertain times.

You will need:
A small black dog figure or image
A piece of smoky quartz or amethyst for clarity
A candle (white or purple)

Light the candle and hold the stone in your hand. Please close your eyes and picture the Black Dog walking beside you, its eyes glowing with wisdom, its presence steady and calm.

"Hecate, I call upon you in your form as the Black Dog. Lead me through the darkness, guide me through uncertainty. As you walk between worlds, could you help me to find my way? Show me the path I am meant to walk and guard me as I move forward."

Carry the stone with you as a reminder of Hecate's guidance, and place the black dog figure on your altar to symbolize her presence in your life.

Chapter 12: The Feast of the Dogs

In ancient Greece, the last day of the month was often considered sacred to Hecate, and offerings of food—especially to her hounds—were left at the crossroads. Known as the **Deipnon**, or Hecate's Supper, this was a time to honor the goddess and her dogs and thank them for their protection and guidance.
On this day, followers of Hecate would leave meals of meat, garlic, and honey at the crossroads, not only as offerings to the goddess but as food for the wandering spirits and her loyal hounds.
"You must remember them," she says. "For they are always watching, always protecting. Honor them, and they will never leave your side."

A Feast for the Hounds

To honor Hecate and her hounds, you can create a feast in their name. This can be done at home, an altar, or a crossroads where their energy is most vital.

You will need:

Meat (cooked or raw)

Garlic cloves

Honey or bread dipped in honey

A bowl of fresh water

A key symbolizing Hecate's presence

Arrange the offerings on a plate and set them at your chosen location. As you place the *offerings, say:*

"Hecate and your sacred hounds, I offer this meal in your honor. I thank you for your protection, for your guidance, and for the strength you have given me. May this food nourish your hounds, and may they always guard my path."

Leave the offering without looking back, trusting that the goddess and her loyal companions will receive it.

With the hounds of Hecate now introduced, we've explored her deep connections to protection, the crossroads, and guidance through the unknown.

The dogs are:

An extension of her power.

Offering fierce loyalty.

Helping those who follow her path face their fate with courage.

Chapter 13: Hecate, Goddess of Witches

The moon is complete now, and the air hums with unseen energy. You stand at your altar, surrounded by herbs, stones, and the tools of your craft. Hecate's presence is strong here, for she is the goddess of witches who taught humanity the sacred arts of magic. Her torches burn brightly at night, illuminating the ancient ways of spellcraft, potion-making, and divination.

"You are a witch," she says, her eyes gleaming in the moonlight. "And you are mine."

Hecate's connection to witchcraft runs deep. She is the goddess who stands at the threshold between the seen and unseen worlds, and through her guidance, witches gain their power. She offers wisdom, protection, and the keys to the mysteries of the universe.

A Dedication Ritual to Hecate as Goddess of Witches

If you seek to walk the path of the witch under Hecate's guidance, a formal dedication can strengthen your bond with her. This ritual will help you declare your intent and ask for her support as you grow in your magical practice.

You will need:

A black or red candle

A key, symbolizing Hecate's role as keeper of the mysteries

A piece of jewelry or a talisman to wear as a sign of your dedication

A bowl of salt water for purification

Begin by purifying yourself with the saltwater, sprinkling it over your hands and face while saying:

"Hecate, cleanse me of all that holds me back. Purify my spirit and prepare me for this dedication."

Light the candle and hold the key in your hands. Close your eyes and feel Hecate's presence around you. When you are ready, say:

"Hecate, Queen of Witches, I dedicate myself to you. I seek your guidance, wisdom, and protection as I walk the path of magic. With this key, I open the door to your mysteries. With this candle, I light the way to deeper knowledge. I am yours, and I ask that you walk with me."

Hold the talisman in your hands and let it absorb the energy of your dedication. Once the ritual is complete, wear it to symbolize your connection to Hecate. Let the candle burn down, and place the key on your altar as a reminder of your promise.

Chapter 14: The Sacred Herbs of Hecate

Hecate is not just the goddess of magic but also of the earth and its sacred plants. As the protector of herbalists and healers, she teaches the power of nature's remedies and the ancient practice of herbal magic. Many plants are sacred to her, each carrying its magical properties, and with her guidance, you can learn how to work with them in your craft.

"The earth holds many secrets," she says, her hands brushing over the plants. "And I will teach you how to unlock them."

67

Hecate's Sacred Herbs

Here are a few of the most sacred herbs associated with Hecate, each one offering a different type of magic:

- **Yew**: Associated with death and rebirth, yew is a powerful herb for working with the spirits and for transformative magic.
- **Garlic**: Used for protection, garlic wards off evil and negativity. It is also a sacred offering to Hecate.
- **Mugwort**: A visionary herb, mugwort is often used in dream magic and divination. It enhances psychic abilities and helps connect to the spirit world.
- **Dittany of Crete**: A powerful herb for astral travel and spirit communication, it is often burned as incense to call upon Hecate during rituals.

A Potion of Protection

This simple potion can be made to protect yourself or your home from negativity and unwanted energies. It uses Hecate's sacred herbs to draw upon her strength and shield you from harm.

You will need:
A sprig of rosemary (for purification)
A clove of garlic (for protection)
A handful of mugwort (for psychic strength)
A black bowl of water

Start by placing the bowl of water on your altar. Crush the garlic, rosemary, and mugwort, releasing their oils and fragrance. As you do so, call upon Hecate:

"Hecate, Keeper of the Threshold, I ask for your protection. Bless these herbs with your strength and shield me from all harm."

Add the herbs to the water bowl, stirring it clockwise three times. Dip your fingers into the potion and anoint your forehead, your heart, and your hands. Say:

"By Hecate's power, I am protected. No harm shall come to me, for her light guards my path."

Use this potion to anoint doors, windows, or any space that needs protection. It can also be used in personal protection rituals before journeying into spiritual work.

Chapter 15: Divination in Hecate's Light

Hecate has long been associated with divination, mainly through the use of the night and the moon's phases. As the torchbearer, she lights the way for those seeking to see beyond the veil of this world into the mysteries of the future. Whether through scrying, tarot, or other forms of divination, Hecate is the guide who illuminates the hidden path.

"Look into the darkness," she says, her voice steady and sure. "There is always something to be seen.

Moon Magic and Scrying

The moon is one of Hecate's most sacred symbols, and its phases are deeply tied to her magic. Scrying by moonlight is one of the simplest yet most powerful forms of divination under Hecate's guidance. This involves gazing into a reflective surface, such as water or a mirror, and allowing images to form in your mind's eye.

You will need:

A black bowl filled with water

A silver candle to represent the moon

A small piece of moonstone or quartz (optional)

Begin by lighting the silver candle and placing it next to the water bowl. Hold the moonstone in your hand, if you are using one, and call upon Hecate:

"Hecate, She of the Crossroads, light my way. Help me to see what is hidden and to understand what lies beyond."

Gaze into the water, letting your mind relax. As you stare at the surface, allow images to form in the ripples or reflections. You may see shapes, symbols, or colors that carry meaning for your question or situation. Take your time; when you feel ready, close your eyes and let the images settle.

Afterward, write down any impressions or messages you received. Hecate often speaks through subtle imagery, so pay attention to your intuition and dreams in the days following the ritual.

Chapter 16: Hecate's Tarot Spread

Another powerful way to connect with Hecate's wisdom is through tarot cards. Hecate's energy is well-suited to deep, introspective readings that explore hidden truths and the journey through transitions. Inspired by Hecate's three faces, this tarot spread will help uncover what lies in the shadows and guide you through personal transformation.

THE PATH
BEHIND YOU

THE
CROSSROADS

HECATE'S
GUIDANCE

The Crossroads Spread

This is a three-card spread designed to reveal your choices, obstacles, and Hecate's guidance to help you make the right decision.

The First Card – The Path Behind You: This card represents your origins. It reflects your past experiences and the energies that have led you to the crossroads.

The Second Card – The Crossroads: This card shows your current choice. It represents the current challenge or opportunity and the forces at play in your decision.

The Third Card – Hecate's Guidance: This card offers insight from Hecate on how to proceed. It may suggest a path forward or illuminate a hidden truth you must consider.

Chapter 17: Hecate's Torches of Illumination

The path is dark, the world around you shadowed and unknown. But in the distance, you see the soft glow of light. As you walk toward it, the darkness recedes, revealing Hecate standing tall, her arms outstretched. In each hand, she holds a blazing torch, their flames flickering but steady, lighting the way forward.

"My torches have always been with you," she says. "Even when the night is darkest, I am here to show you the path."

Hecate's torches symbolize more than just light — they represent knowledge, clarity, and the ability to see through the veil of illusion. She is the goddess who guides us through the darkest moments of our lives, offering illumination in the face of fear and uncertainty. Her torches light the way not only for those crossing between worlds but also for those seeking truth within themselves.

The Light in the Darkness

Hecate's dual torches are often depicted as the light that guides travelers and souls through the realms of the underworld, where she reigns as Queen. Her torches symbolize the illumination of knowledge and wisdom — particularly the kind of wisdom that can only be gained by walking through the dark places of the soul.

"When the way forward is unclear," she says, "when fear grips your heart, and you do not know where to turn, call upon my torches. I will light your path."

A Ritual to Invoke Hecate's Torches

This ritual calls upon Hecate's torches when you need clarity, guidance, or protection. Whether facing a difficult decision or navigating a period of uncertainty, her torches can help light the way forward.

You will need:

Two white or black candles (to represent Hecate's torches)

A key (to symbolize her role as a gatekeeper)

A small mirror (to reflect the light of the torches)

A dark cloth or veil

Begin by placing the two candles on either side of your altar, symbolizing Hecate's dual torches. Place the key in the center between them, and lay the mirror in front of you. Drape the dark cloth or veil over your head, symbolizing the darkness you seek to understand.

Light the candles and say:

"Hecate, Keeper of the Flame, I call upon you now. Light the way through the darkness, and guide me with your wisdom. As your torches blaze, so too shall the truth be revealed."

Gaze into the mirror, watching as the candlelight reflects off its surface. Take a few deep breaths and focus on the flickering flames, allowing yourself to slip into a meditative state. As you do, visualize Hecate standing before you, her torches blazing at night. Ask her for the guidance or clarity you need, and allow any images, thoughts, or feelings to arise.

Once you feel you have received your answer, thank Hecate and extinguish the candles. Keep the key on your altar as a reminder that her light is always with you, even in the darkest times.

Chapter 18: The Flame of Inner Wisdom

As Hecate's torches illuminate the path through physical and spiritual darkness, they also reveal the hidden truths within ourselves. Her light represents the flame of inner wisdom, aiding us in recognizing the aspects of ourselves that we may have concealed or overlooked. This facet of Hecate's power may not always be comfortable, as it compels us to confront our fears, shadows, and deepest desires. However, in doing so, it empowers us to grow.

"You cannot hide from yourself," Hecate says, her torches held high. "For I will always see what lies within. And if you have the courage to look, you will see it too."

Her torches burn with the light of truth and the flame of transformation. When we walk with Hecate, we are asked to see ourselves clearly and to accept the reality of who we are — both our strengths and our weaknesses.

A Prayer for Inner Wisdom

You can offer her this prayer to invoke Hecate's torches in your journey of self-discovery. It is a call for her to light the way within, helping you uncover the hidden parts of your soul and the wisdom that resides there.

You will need:

A single white candle (for clarity)

A small key or charm to hold during the prayer

Light the candle and hold the key in your hands. Please close your eyes and visualize Hecate standing before you, her torches blazing brightly.

Say:

"Hecate, Bearer of the Flame, shine your light within me. Please help me to clearly see the truth about who I am. Reveal the wisdom that lies hidden in the dark, and guide me to embrace all parts of myself. I trust in your light, O Great Hecate, to show me the way."

Hold the key tightly in your hand, letting it absorb the energy of the prayer. Afterward, you can carry the key with you as a reminder that Hecate's light is always there to guide you.

Chapter 19: The Torches and the Crossroads

Hecate's torches are particularly significant at the crossroads, where she stands as the guardian and gatekeeper. The crossroads is a place of decision, transformation, and new beginnings, and it is here that her torches burn the brightest. When you find yourself at a metaphorical or literal crossroads in life, Hecate's light can show you the way forward.

"There is always a choice to be made," she says, her torches flickering in the night. "But do not fear the crossroads, for I am there with you."

In many magical traditions, the crossroads is a place of power, and for those who walk Hecate's path, it is sacred ground. Her torches not only illuminate the choices before us but also guide us safely through times of transition and change.

A Crossroads Ritual for Clarity

When faced with a difficult decision or a moment of transition, you can call upon Hecate's torches at the crossroads to help you see the best path forward. This ritual can be performed at a literal crossroads or your altar, using representations of the crossroads.

You will need:

Two candles to represent Hecate's torches

A small key or coin to leave as an offering at the crossroads

A bowl of water (to symbolize the flowing of time and change)

Begin by lighting the two candles and placing them on either side of the bowl of water. Hold the key or coin in your hand and say:

"Hecate, Guardian of the Crossroads, I stand at the threshold of change. Light the way forward with your torches, and guide me through this time of uncertainty. Help me to see the path that is right for me."

Gaze into the bowl of water, watching how the light of the candles reflects off its surface. As you do, ask Hecate for guidance in your decision. You may receive a clear answer in the form of a thought, image, or feeling, or you may feel a sense of peace and clarity about the choice ahead.

When you are ready, leave the key or coin at a crossroads or a sacred place as an offering to Hecate, thanking her for her guidance.

"Through her symbols, the mysteries are revealed. Each key unlocks a door, each torch guides the way, and each step brings the seeker closer to truth."

Chapter 20: The Eternal Flame

While Hecate's torches represent guidance and protection, they also symbolize the eternal flame — the light of life that continues even through death and rebirth. As a goddess of both life and death, Hecate's flame burns in all worlds, reminding us that even in the darkest times, the light endures.

"The flame never dies," Hecate whispers, her torches glowing softly. "It only changes. Through death, through transformation, through time itself, my light remains."

Her torches teach us that there is always hope, always a path forward, no matter how dark things may seem. In the cycle of life and death, her flame represents the continuity of existence and the constant flow of energy between worlds.

A Meditation on the Eternal Flame

This meditation is designed to connect you with Hecate's eternal flame, helping you find hope and strength during times of difficulty or loss. It reminds you that no matter how dark things may become, her light is always with you.

You will need:

A candle to represent Hecate's flame (black, white, or red)

A tranquil area where you can relax without any interruptions. Light the candle and sit comfortably. Close your eyes and focus on your breath, allowing yourself to relax. Visualize the flame of the candle growing brighter, expanding to fill the space around you. As the flame grows, it becomes Hecate's torch, burning brightly in the darkness. See Hecate standing before you, her torches blazing. Experience the comforting glow of her radiance and the power it bestows upon you. Let her fire instill you with optimism, bravery, and the understanding that you have the ability to conquer any obstacle."

When you are ready, open your eyes and take a deep breath, knowing that Hecate's flame will continue to burn within you, even after the candle is extinguished.

This chapter highlights the significance of Hecate's torches in guiding us through darkness, whether it be physical, emotional, or spiritual. Her torches symbolize wisdom, clarity, and the ability to find our way through even the most challenging times.

Chapter 21: Creating Hecate's Altar

Building an altar for Hecate is a sacred act that honors her presence in your life and invites her wisdom, protection, and power into your space. Hecate's altar is a focal point for rituals, offerings, and personal connection. It's a place where you can reflect, meditate, and perform magic under her guidance.

"You must create a space that reflects your devotion," Hecate says, her eyes steady and intense. "A space where I may stand with you, where the flames of my torches may burn."

The Elements of Hecate's Altar

When constructing an altar for Hecate, your chosen items should reflect her power and symbolism. There are several key elements that are traditionally included on an altar dedicated to Hecate, but it's important to remember that your altar should also be a personal expression of your relationship with her.

Here are some traditional and suggested items to include:

1. **Torches or Candles**: Hecate is often depicted holding torches, so placing two candles on the altar symbolizes her role as a guide through the darkness. You can use black, white, or red candles, depending on your intent or the phase of the moon.

2. **Keys**: Hecate is the Keeper of Keys, symbolizing her ability to unlock doors between worlds and offer guidance through transitions. A key (or multiple keys) on your altar honors this aspect of her power. Antique or skeleton keys are particularly resonant, but any key that holds personal meaning can be used.

3. **A Bowl of Water or Black Mirror**: Hecate is also associated with scrying and divination. A bowl of water or a black mirror can represent her ability to see through the veil and into the hidden realms.

4. **Herbs**: Sacred herbs associated with Hecate, such as

mugwort, garlic, and yew, can be placed on her altar. You can also use rosemary for purification or lavender for protection.

5. **Dogs or Dog Figures**: As the goddess is often accompanied by her sacred hounds, a small statue or image of a black dog can symbolize their role as her protectors and companions.

6. **Offerings**: Traditional offerings include food, such as eggs, garlic, bread, honey, wine, or pomegranates. These can be placed on the altar during rituals or left at a crossroads to honor her.

7. **Skulls or Bones**: A small animal skull or bone can symbolize Hecate's connection to death, the underworld, and transformation, representing her power over life and death.

8. **A Keyhole or Door Symbol**: To represent her role as the gatekeeper, you should place a keyhole, door, or small representation of a doorway on the altar, symbolizing her ability to open the paths between worlds.

Steps to Building the Altar

1. **Choose a Location**: Select a quiet, undisturbed space for Hecate's altar. This could be a table, shelf, or small corner where you feel connected to her energy. Since Hecate is associated with liminal spaces, consider placing her altar near an entrance, crossroads, or window, symbolically representing thresholds.

2. **Cleanse the Space**: Before you begin setting up the altar, cleanse the space using sacred herbs such as mugwort, sage, or rosemary. As you cleanse, call upon Hecate to bless the space and open the way for her presence to reside.

3. **Arrange the Items with Intention**: Place each item on the altar thoughtfully, as each object symbolizes an aspect of Hecate's power. For example, you might place the candles or torches on either side of the altar to represent her dual flames. The keys can rest at the center, symbolizing her role as a guide and gatekeeper.

4. **Add Personal Touches**: Your altar should reflect your relationship with Hecate. Feel free to add items that hold special meaning for you, such as crystals, personal talismans, or objects that remind you of her presence.

5. **Make Offerings Regularly**: Offerings are essential to maintaining a relationship with Hecate. You can leave food offerings on the altar and later bring them to a crossroads or

another sacred space. Regular offerings of wine, honey, and garlic will honor her and maintain her favor.

"To create an altar for Hecate is to build a bridge between worlds, a sacred space where light and shadow meet, and where the goddess watches over her own."

Chapter 22: Sharing Hecate's Altar

Sharing an altar between deities can be a sensitive topic, especially when working with a powerful goddess like Hecate. While she is not possessive, she is particular about who she shares her sacred space with. Certain deities align well with Hecate's energy, while others may conflict with her power, depending on their roles and realms of influence.

Deities That Align Well with Hecate

Hecate is known for her versatility, and she can share her altar with deities who complement her energies, particularly those connected to the underworld, death, magic, or the moon. Some deities that align well with Hecate include:

Persephone: As the Queen of the Underworld, Persephone shares a deep connection with Hecate. Their roles as guides through the underworld and their association with death, rebirth, and transformation make them harmonious on the same altar.

Hermes: Both Hecate and Hermes serve as psychopomps, leading souls from the realm of the living to the realm of the dead. They work well together, particularly in matters of communication, magic, and transitions.

Selene: As a lunar goddess, Selene's connection with the moon aligns with Hecate's own lunar aspects. The pairing of their energies enhances rituals involving the cycles of the moon, night magic, and protection.

Hel: The Norse goddess of death and the underworld shares many traits with Hecate, particularly in their roles as keepers of the dead. Their energies complement each other, particularly in rituals involving death, transformation, and ancestral magic.

Anubis: The Egyptian god of mummification and the afterlife aligns well with Hecate, as both are guardians of the dead and guide the transition between life and death.

Deities Best Kept Separate

While Hecate can share her altar with other deities, some are best kept separate due to conflicting energies or roles that may not align with her magic. These deities include:

Solar Deities: Hecate's domain is the night, the moon, and the shadow realms. Deities associated with the sun, such as Apollo, Ra, or Helios, may have energies that clash with Hecate's darker, more mysterious aspects. It's best to keep their altars separate, especially if you focus on night magic or underworld workings.

Deities of Pure Light: Deities purely associated with light, such as certain aspects of angels or figures of pure goodness, may conflict with Hecate's dual nature of light and dark. Her energy balances between realms and an altar dedicated to only light forces may not resonate with her transformative and shadow-working magic.

War Deities: Hecate's power is not one of direct combat or destruction. While she can defend and protect fiercely, deities of war and violence, such as Ares or Mars, do not typically align well with her subtle, liminal powers of protection and magic.

Creating a Harmonious
Shared Altar

Include other deities on your altar with Hecate to ensure a harmonious balance between their energies. Here are some guidelines for creating a shared space:

Separate Spaces: You can create separate spaces for each deity, even on the same altar. For example, Hecate's tools and offerings can be placed on one side, while the other deity's items are on the opposite side. This honors each entity's space and power without causing overlap.

1. **Complementary Offerings**: When sharing an altar, offer foods or items that honor both deities, such as wine, bread, or sacred herbs. These offerings can be accepted by both Hecate and the deity you are working with.
2. **Check for Signs**: When setting up a shared altar, pay attention to signs from Hecate and the other deities. If offerings go untouched or you feel uncomfortable around the altar, it may be a sign that the energies are clashing, and a separation may be necessary.

This chapter covers the essentials of building and maintaining a dedicated altar for Hecate and the etiquette of sharing her space with other deities. This will allow practitioners to create a sacred place where Hecate's energy can be honored fully, and her powers can work in harmony with others.

Would you like to explore more profound rituals connected to her altar or another aspect of her practice next?

Chapter 23: The Sacred Symbols of Hecate

Symbols have always been powerful conduits of magic and meaning, and Hecate's symbols are no exception. Each one represents a facet of her complex nature as a goddess of magic, the underworld, the moon, and the crossroads. To truly understand Hecate, one must also understand the significance of the symbols she holds dear.

As you walk further on Hecate's path, these symbols will begin to reveal their power in your life. You'll see them in dreams, find them in nature, or feel their pull in the moments when you need her the most.

"They are the keys to my mysteries," Hecate says, her voice soft but filled with authority. "They are how I speak to those who are ready to listen."

105

Key Symbols of Hecate

Here are the most significant symbols associated with Hecate, each carrying its own layer of meaning and power:

1. The Key

The key is Hecate's most iconic symbol, representing her role as the **Keeper of the Keys**. She holds the keys to the realms of the living, the dead, and the divine. With these keys, she unlocks the doors between worlds, guiding souls through transitions and offering knowledge to those who seek it.

Meaning: The key symbolizes access to hidden knowledge, transitions, and the ability to open or close doors in life, both literal and metaphorical. It also represents her role as a guardian of thresholds and the gates of the underworld.

How to Use: Keep a key on your altar or wear one as a charm to invoke Hecate's guidance and protection, especially during times of transition or when seeking hidden knowledge. Use keys in rituals that involve seeking a new path, unlocking mysteries, or calling upon Hecate to open the way forward.

2. The Torches

Hecate's torches symbolize **illumination and guidance through darkness**. As the torchbearer, she lights the way for those navigating the shadowy realms, offering clarity when the path is unclear. Her torches are also used to protect and guide souls through the underworld.

Meaning: The torches symbolize clarity, wisdom, and the ability to see through the veil of darkness and mystery. They represent spiritual light, guiding the seeker through the unknown.

How to Use: Candles represent her torches in ritual. Light two candles to symbolize her dual flames when asking for her guidance in times of uncertainty or when seeking clarity on your spiritual path. Use them to illuminate the truth, protect you from unseen dangers, or call her to your aid.

3. The Dogs

Hecate's sacred hounds are powerful protectors, guardians of the crossroads, and guides for lost souls. These black dogs are loyal companions to Hecate, and their presence is a reminder that she is always watching over those who walk her path.

Meaning: Dogs are seen as symbols of protection, loyalty, and guardianship. They also represent Hecate's association with the underworld and her role as a guide for souls to the afterlife.

How to Use: Place images or statues of black dogs on your altar to honor Hecate's hounds and invoke their protective presence. You can also work with their energy to protect your home, guide you through spiritual journeys, or connect with the spirits of the dead.

4. The Crossroads

The crossroads is one of the most important symbols of Hecate, representing the meeting point between worlds, decisions, and transitions. Hecate is often depicted standing at a crossroads, where she guides travelers and souls, offering wisdom on which path to take.

Meaning: The crossroads symbolize choices, transitions, and the liminal spaces between life and death, past and future. It's a place of great power where decisions are made and new paths are opened.

How to Use: Use the crossroads symbolically or literally in rituals when you are at a pivotal point in life, need to decide, or seek new opportunities. You can visit a physical crossroads to make offerings to Hecate, asking for her guidance on which path to take.

5. The Dagger

Hecate is often depicted with a dagger or athame, symbolizing her power over life and death. The dagger is a tool of protection, cutting away illusions and barriers. It also represents her role as a goddess of magic and witchcraft, used in rituals to direct energy and perform sacred acts.

Meaning: The dagger represents protection, power, and the ability to cut through obstacles or illusions. It symbolizes magical control and the ability to direct energy with precision.

How to Use: Use a dagger or athame in rituals to protect yourself, clear away negative energy, or symbolically cut ties with the past. It can also be used to trace protective circles or direct energy during spellwork.

6. The Serpent

Hecate is often associated with the serpent, symbolizing **transformation, rebirth, and wisdom**. The serpent sheds its skin, symbolizing the cycle of life, death, and renewal. As a goddess of the underworld, Hecate uses the serpent's wisdom to guide those who seek transformation.

Meaning: The serpent symbolizes transformation, rebirth, and the wisdom of change. It is also connected to the earth, representing the hidden knowledge of nature and the cycles of life.

How to Use: Incorporate serpent imagery or symbolism into your practice when undergoing personal transformation or seeking to release old patterns. The serpent's energy can help you navigate complex changes and emerge stronger on the other side.

7. The Crescent Moon

Hecate is deeply connected to the moon, particularly the dark moon and its crescent phase. The crescent moon symbolizes the cycle of life, death, and rebirth—the continuous flow of time. During the dark moon, Hecate's power is most potent when her torches illuminate the hidden realms of the soul.

Meaning: The crescent moon symbolizes transitions, new beginnings, and the hidden wisdom of the night. It represents Hecate's dominion over the lunar cycles and her power as a goddess of magic and the night.

How to Use: Align your rituals with the phases of the moon to work with Hecate's energy. The dark moon is a potent time to connect with her for introspection, shadow work, or divination. Use crescent moon symbols in rituals for new beginnings and spiritual growth.

8. The Triple-Headed Form

One of the most potent symbols of Hecate is her **triple-headed form**, often depicted as a woman with three faces. This represents her dominion over the past, present, and future and her ability to see in all directions at once. The triple form reflects her roles as Maiden, Mother, and Crone.

Meaning: The triple form symbolizes Hecate's omniscience, her ability to navigate the realms of time, and her connection to the three phases of womanhood and life: birth, life, and death.

How to Use: In your practice, use triple symbols or representations of Hecate to connect with her wisdom across time. The triple goddess aspect can be invoked when seeking guidance about the past, present, or future or when working through transitions in your own life.

Chapter 24: Incorporating Hecate's Symbols into Rituals

Once you understand Hecate's symbols, the next step is learning how to use them in your practice. Each symbol carries its own magical energy and can be incorporated into rituals, meditations, or daily devotions to Hecate.

A Ritual of Symbolic Invocation

This ritual is designed to invoke Hecate's presence by calling upon her key symbols, combining their power to create a deep connection with the goddess.

You will need:

A key (for unlocking hidden knowledge)

Two candles (for her torches)

A small bowl of water (representing the crossroads or divination)

A dog figurine or image (for protection)

A dagger or sharp object (for cutting away obstacles)

Begin by lighting the two candles and placing the key between them on your altar. Hold the dog figurine and say:

"Hecate, Guardian of the Threshold, I call upon you now. With your hounds at my side, protect me as I walk your path."

Next, hold the key and say:

"Hecate, Keeper of Keys, unlock the doors of wisdom and show me the hidden paths. I seek your guidance and your light."

Gaze into the bowl of water, allowing the light of the candles to reflect on its surface. Say:

"Hecate, the Torchbearer, lights the way through the darkness. With your flame, I see the path ahead."

Finally, hold the dagger or sharp object and say:

"Hecate, Mistress of Magic, with your power, I cut away all that holds me back. Guide me through this transformation, and help me become what I am meant to be."

Spend a few moments in silence, feeling Hecate's presence around you. Let her symbols fill the space with their power. When you are ready, extinguish the candles and thank Hecate for her guidance.

This chapter has explored Hecate's most powerful and direct symbols, their meanings, and how to incorporate them into rituals and daily practice. These symbols offer a way to connect deeply with Hecate's many aspects and invite her presence into your life.

Chapter 25: The Sacred Path of Hecate's Followers

As the journey comes to a close, one truth becomes clear: Hecate sees her followers as sacred. To walk her path is to be embraced by her dark and powerful energy, but it also means being fiercely protected. Hecate is not a goddess who watches passively from afar—she is ever-present, her torches burning brightly at your side, her hounds at your feet, and her wisdom guiding you through every crossroads. "To follow me is to be set apart," Hecate says, her voice firm but filled with a deep sense of care. "You are mine, and I do not abandon my own."

Hecate's Protection: The Fierce Guardian

Hecate is known as a **goddess of protection**, particularly for those who walk between worlds or who find themselves navigating the darker, more mysterious paths of life. Her followers are often those who seek transformation, wisdom, and a deeper understanding of the unseen. In return, she offers fierce protection, guiding them through the darkest nights and ensuring no harm befalls them as they walk her sacred path.

"There are forces in this world," she says, "that seek to tear down what you build, to silence your voice, and to dim your flame. But I will not allow it. Under my protection, you are safe."

Hecate protects not only the body but also the spirit. She shields her followers from those who would seek to harm them, be it through malice, jealousy, or ignorance. For those who dedicate themselves to her, Hecate's defense is unyielding, and her loyalty is without question.

The Sacred Oath

For those who choose to walk with Hecate, there is an unspoken oath between the goddess and the follower. This oath is not one of blind obedience but of mutual respect. Hecate offers her wisdom and protection, and in return, she asks for reverence, truth, and the courage to face the unknown.

"Hear me," she says, her torches blazing in the night. "If you walk with me, you must walk with strength, for I do not lead the fearful. I lead the brave, the seekers of truth, and those who are unafraid to see what lies beyond."

Walking Hecate's Path: Who Should Follow

Hecate does not call to everyone, but those who hear her call feel it deeply, like an echo from a past life or a whisper in their soul. Those who walk Hecate's path are often drawn to the mysteries of life and death, the liminal spaces between worlds, and the pursuit of wisdom that lies hidden in the shadows.

This path is not for the faint-hearted. It requires strength, curiosity, and a willingness to face both the light and the dark within yourself. Hecate does not demand perfection from her followers, but she does require honesty and a desire to grow. Those who walk with her must be prepared to face their fears, confront their shadows, and embrace the power of transformation.

The Qualities of Hecate's Followers

There are certain qualities that Hecate looks for in her followers, those whom she takes under her protection and guides along her path:

Courage: Hecate's path is one of transformation and growth, often requiring her followers to confront difficult truths. Hecate values those who dare to face these challenges head-on, trusting in her guidance to lead them through.

Honesty: Hecate is a goddess who sees through deception, both from others and within ourselves. Her followers must be honest with themselves, willing to look at their own flaws, desires, and fears without turning away.

Wisdom: Hecate's followers are seekers of truth. They are not content with surface-level answers but strive to understand the deeper mysteries of the universe. Hecate rewards those who seek wisdom and knowledge with her insights and guidance.

Resilience: Life is full of trials, and Hecate's followers are often those who have been through darkness and emerged stronger. They are resilient and able to adapt and grow even in the face of adversity.

Empathy: Though Hecate is a goddess of the crossroads and the underworld, she is also a protector of those who are lost or in need. Her followers often share this trait, offering guidance and empathy to others who find themselves at a crossroads in life.

How to Walk Hecate's Path

1. **Walking on Hecate's path** involves progressing with reverence, responsibility, and a deep acknowledgment of the sacredness of the journey. It is not just about casting spells and performing rituals; it requires a lifelong dedication to change, wisdom, and protection. Here are some fundamental guidelines for following this path: Show respect at the Crossroads: The crossroads hold great significance for Hecate, both symbolically and literally. Show respect by making offerings, contemplating your decisions, and seeking Hecate's guidance during times of transition. Embrace the Darkness: Hecate teaches that there is wisdom in the darkness, and it should not be feared. Engage in shadow work, confront your inner fears, and trust Hecate will guide you through challenging times. Pursue Knowledge: Hecate is the goddess of wisdom and magic, and her followers should always strive to expand their knowledge and understanding. Commit to learning and personal growth through study, self-reflection, or spiritual practices.

2. **Offer Devotion**: Hecate appreciates offerings and rituals performed in her name. These can be simple gestures, such as lighting a candle, leaving food at a crossroads, or more elaborate ceremonies of dedication and prayer. The key is sincerity in your devotion.

3. **Protect the Vulnerable**: Just as Hecate fiercely protects her followers, so too must her followers stand up for those who are vulnerable. Whether through spiritual protection, emotional support, or practical aid, be a guardian to those in need.

4. **Honor the Dead**: As a goddess of the underworld, Hecate's path is closely tied to death and the spirits of the dead. Honor your ancestors, perform rituals of remembrance, and show respect to those who have passed.

The Path of Sacred Devotion

To be one of Hecate's followers is to walk a sacred path of devotion, wisdom, and protection. She does not promise an easy journey, but she promises a meaningful one. For those who dare to follow her, the rewards are great: her protection is fierce, her wisdom is boundless, and her presence is deeply transformative.

"You are sacred to me," Hecate says, her voice filled with power. "And I will guard you as my own."

When you walk with Hecate, you are never alone. Her torches will light your way, her hounds will guard your steps, and her wisdom will guide you through every challenge. She will stand beside you at every crossroad, offering the strength and protection you need to continue on your journey.

Final Prayer: A Call to Hecate
Hecate, Keeper of the Keys,

125

Guardian of the Crossroads,
I call upon you now,
You who stand at the threshold of all worlds.
Torchbearer, light my path when the way is unclear,
Guide me through the shadows,
And grant me the wisdom to see beyond the veil of night.
You who hold the secrets of life, death, and rebirth,
Teach me to walk your path with courage and grace,
To embrace the light and the dark,
To face my fears and transform through your power.
As I stand at the crossroads,
May your dogs protect me,
May your keys unlock the doors to my highest self,
And may your torches always light my way.
In your name, I honor the wisdom of the Maiden,
The strength of the Mother,
And the deep knowing of the Crone.
Hecate, Queen of Witches,
Guardian of the Night,
I offer this prayer in gratitude,
For your protection, your guidance, and your love.
May I walk with you,
Now and always,
As your sacred follower,
And as one who seeks your light in the dark.
So mote it be.

A Special Note to My Dearest Husband

To my beloved husband, Louis, this journey would not have been possible without you by my side. Your unwavering support, love, and encouragement have been the foundation that has allowed me to pursue my passions and dreams. You have stood with me through every crossroad, every challenge, and every transformation, and for that, I am eternally grateful.

Your strength and kindness remind me every day of the power of true partnership. You are my rock, my light, and the love of my life. Thank you for walking this path with me, for believing in me, and for being the best partner anyone could ask for.

With all my love,

Vespera Morrigan

With each seed
a new story begins....

About the Author: Vespera Morrigan

Vespera Morrigan has walked the path of magic for many years, drawing upon the ancient wisdom of the gods and goddesses who guard the unseen realms. As a devoted follower of Hecate, she seeks to illuminate the mysteries of magic, transformation, and the crossroads for others. Vespera lives and breathes the sacred teachings passed down through time, using her craft to help others embrace their own power, wisdom, and connection to the divine. She continues to explore the intricate web of connections between the gods and goddesses, sharing her insights and journey through her writings.

Don't miss out!

Visit the website below and you can sign up to receive emails whenever Vespera Morrigan publishes a new book. There's no charge and no obligation.

https://books2read.com/r/B-A-AYPVC-CFQIF

Connecting independent readers to independent writers.